KU-753-108

TIMOTHY KNAPMAN
RIVER STORIES
ILLUSTRATED BY
ASHLING LINDSAY &
IRENE MONTANO

EGMONT

Brainse Mheal Ráthluirc
Charleville Mall Branch
Tel. 8749619

To Abel and Clevan
with love – T.K.

EGMONT
We bring stories to life

First published in Great Britain 2020 by Egmont UK Limited,
The Yellow Building, 1 Nicholas Road, London W11 4AN
www.egmont.co.uk

Text copyright © Timothy Knapman 2020
Illustrations copyright © Ashling Lindsay and Egmont UK Limited 2020
Illustrated by Ashling Lindsay and Irene Montano

Timothy Knapman and Ashling Lindsay have asserted their moral rights.

ISBN 978 1 4052 9254 2

A CIP catalogue record for this title is available from the British Library.

All rights reserved. No part of this publication may be reproduced,
stored in a retrieval system, or transmitted, in any form or by any
means, electronic, mechanical, photocopying, recording or otherwise,
without the prior permission of the publisher and copyright owner.

Stay safe online. Egmont is not responsible for content hosted by third parties.

Egmont takes its responsibility to the planet and its inhabitants very seriously.
We aim to use papers from well-managed forests run by responsible suppliers.

Rising in the jungle heart of Africa, the Nile is the longest river in the world. For 6,695km, it flows past mysterious forests and towering mountains, sparkling lakes and dusty deserts, as scarlet ibises wheel and soar overhead. The river tumbles down waterfalls and races along rapids until, at last, it empties into the Mediterranean Sea.

Let's journey along this mighty river and learn the legends that were spoken here and the stories that were spun. These are tales of life and death, of people and their gods, of mystery and adventure . . .

MEDITERRANEAN
SEA

EGYPT

SAUDIA
ARABIA

NILE

THE TOWERING PINEAPPLE

Completed in 1961, the 187m Cairo Tower is Egypt's tallest building. Its lattice-work design represents the lotus flower, which symbolized creation and rebirth in ancient Egypt. That hasn't stopped some people saying it looks like a big pineapple!

RAISING A RIVER GOD

A huge statue of Hapi, the god of the Nile, once stood guard at the river's mouth. An earthquake sent it crashing into the sea, where it lay forgotten for more than 2,000 years. Archaeologists raised it from the depths in 2001. Now the god stands upright once more.

MEDITERRANEAN SEA

DOUBLE DISASTER

Adventure-loving writer Ernest Hemingway and his wife Mary were flying over Murchison Falls in 1954 when their plane crashed. They survived and boarded a rescue plane – but, on take-off, that crashed, too! They continued their journey by car.

About 85 per cent of the Nile's water comes from the Ethiopian Highlands.

Kagera River

RWANDA

BURUNDI

UGANDA

TANZANIA   *Lake Victoria*

KENYA

KISUMU

Murchison Falls

FESTIVAL TIME

Music, dance and art events at Kisumu on the shores of Lake Victoria celebrate the river's many cultures. The festivals also warn of the flooding and drought that climate change brings.

White Nile

THE SPIRIT OF THE BLUE NILE

On the first day of the year, Ethiopian farmers throw milk and bread into the river as offerings for its spirits. They believe the river has healing powers and connects all who live by it into one family.

ETHIOPIA

Blue Nile

The Mississippi

Travelling the length of the United States, the Mississippi river supplies water to millions of people, and it is home to more than 1,000 animal species. When its source, Minnesota's Lake Itasca, freezes in winter, the river still flows from it, fed by warm underground springs.

A droplet of water takes three months to journey from the cold lake to the warm waters of the Gulf of Mexico. On our journey, we'll discover stories of adventure and hardship, music and mystery, and a lost city from long ago . . .

CANADA

USA

MISSISSIPPI

MEXICO

GULF OF MEXICO

Brainse Mheal Ráthluirc
Charleville Mall Branch
Tel. 8749619

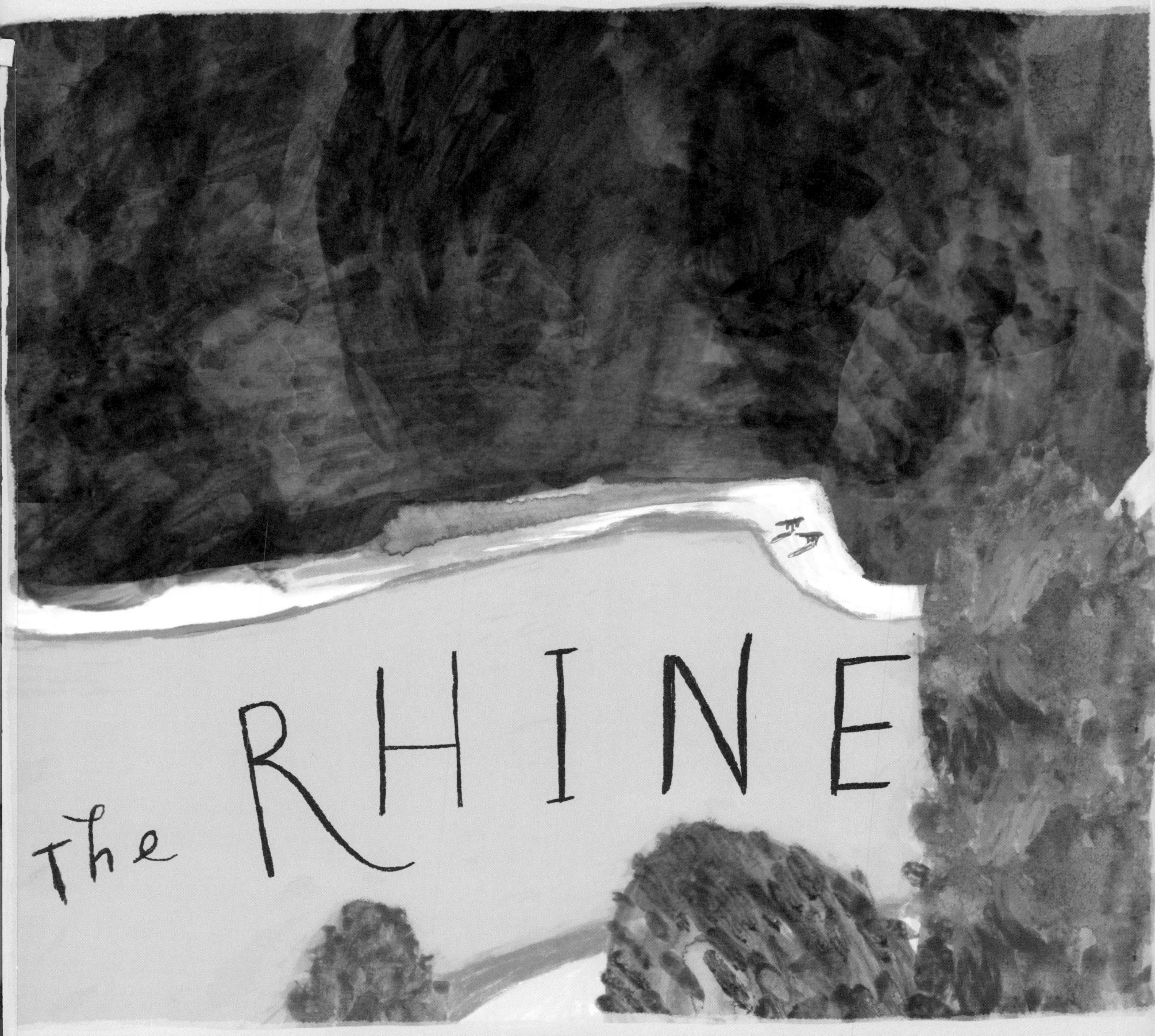
The RHINE

Born in a glacier high in the Swiss Alps, the Rhine,
at first a stream, swells and deepens into sparkling
lakes before crashing over the mighty Rhine Falls.
In Germany, the river's banks are thick with vineyards
and studded with fairytale castles. In the Netherlands, the Rhine fans
out into a fertile delta, bright with summer flowers, and spills into the sea.

We'll follow the Rhine as it twists and turns,
whispering tales of music and magic, heroes and villains –
and brave tribes facing a treacherous journey . . .

NETHERLANDS

RHINE

BELGIUM   GERMANY

FRANCE

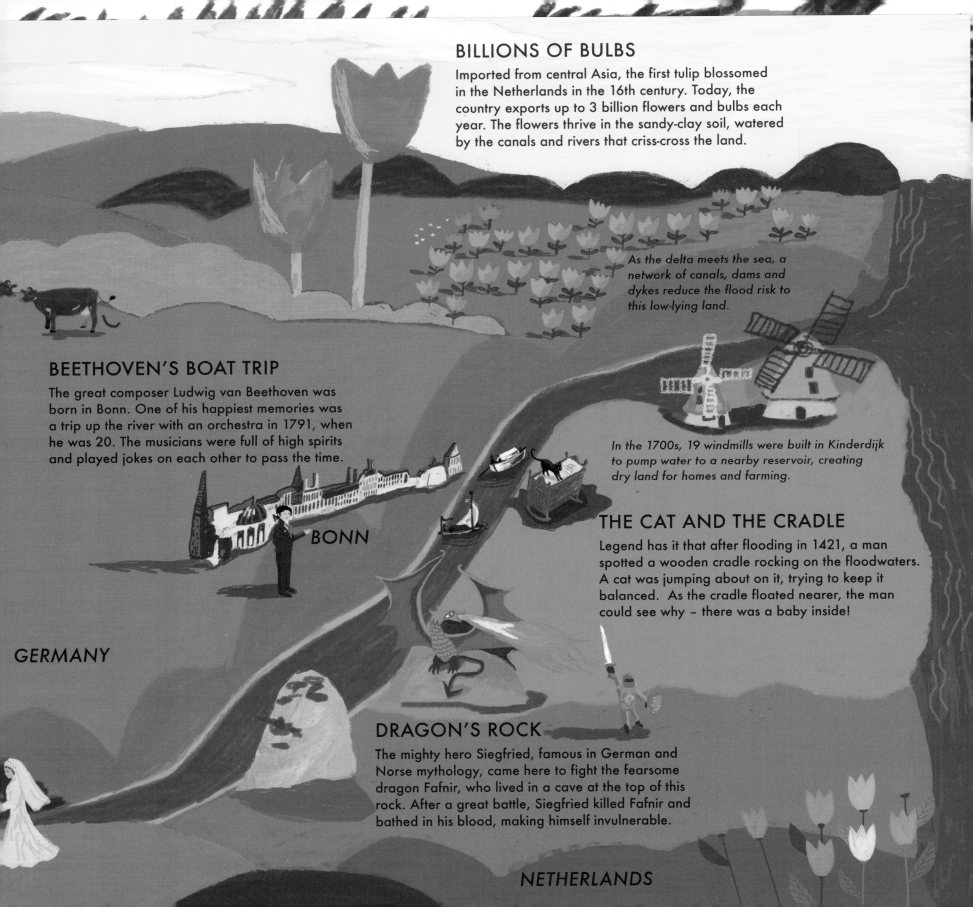

BILLIONS OF BULBS

Imported from central Asia, the first tulip blossomed in the Netherlands in the 16th century. Today, the country exports up to 3 billion flowers and bulbs each year. The flowers thrive in the sandy-clay soil, watered by the canals and rivers that criss-cross the land.

As the delta meets the sea, a network of canals, dams and dykes reduce the flood risk to this low-lying land.

BEETHOVEN'S BOAT TRIP

The great composer Ludwig van Beethoven was born in Bonn. One of his happiest memories was a trip up the river with an orchestra in 1791, when he was 20. The musicians were full of high spirits and played jokes on each other to pass the time.

BONN

In the 1700s, 19 windmills were built in Kinderdijk to pump water to a nearby reservoir, creating dry land for homes and farming.

THE CAT AND THE CRADLE

Legend has it that after flooding in 1421, a man spotted a wooden cradle rocking on the floodwaters. A cat was jumping about on it, trying to keep it balanced. As the cradle floated nearer, the man could see why – there was a baby inside!

GERMANY

DRAGON'S ROCK

The mighty hero Siegfried, famous in German and Norse mythology, came here to fight the fearsome dragon Fafnir, who lived in a cave at the top of this rock. After a great battle, Siegfried killed Fafnir and bathed in his blood, making himself invulnerable.

NETHERLANDS

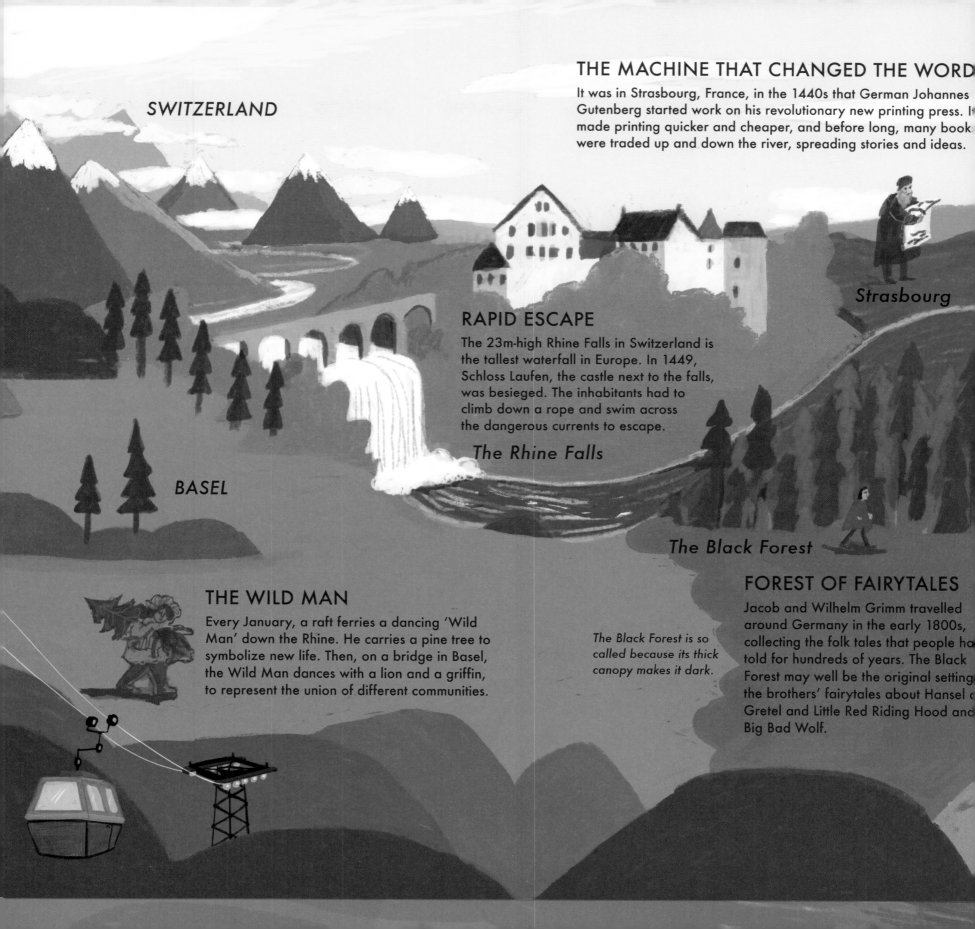

SWITZERLAND

THE MACHINE THAT CHANGED THE WORD

It was in Strasbourg, France, in the 1440s that German Johannes Gutenberg started work on his revolutionary new printing press. It made printing quicker and cheaper, and before long, many book were traded up and down the river, spreading stories and ideas.

Strasbourg

RAPID ESCAPE

The 23m-high Rhine Falls in Switzerland is the tallest waterfall in Europe. In 1449, Schloss Laufen, the castle next to the falls, was besieged. The inhabitants had to climb down a rope and swim across the dangerous currents to escape.

The Rhine Falls

The Black Forest

BASEL

THE WILD MAN

Every January, a raft ferries a dancing 'Wild Man' down the Rhine. He carries a pine tree to symbolize new life. Then, on a bridge in Basel, the Wild Man dances with a lion and a griffin, to represent the union of different communities.

The Black Forest is so called because its thick canopy makes it dark.

FOREST OF FAIRYTALES

Jacob and Wilhelm Grimm travelled around Germany in the early 1800s, collecting the folk tales that people ha told for hundreds of years. The Black Forest may well be the original setting the brothers' fairytales about Hansel Gretel and Little Red Riding Hood and Big Bad Wolf.

The fire dragons scorched the land, leaving trails of flame, smoke and ash.

Wangliang sent an army of 50,000 monsters to fight the dragons. For seven days and seven nights, they battled. When Wangliang was all but defeated, he gathered his remaining forces into two columns and sculpted each one into a red fire dragon.

The green dragon was exhausted after so many days of fighting. But, transforming itself into a river, it fell upon one of the fire dragons, extinguishing it forever. Wounded by the struggle, the green dragon did not get up. Instead – just as the yellow dragon became the Yellow River – the green dragon became the Yangtze.

Now we've seen the river formed, let's dip into its ancient waters to find more tales of myth and magic . . .

THE BATTLE OF THE GREEN DRAGON

Forty-five million years ago in what is now Tibet, small streams emerged from a glacier and, over time, formed a mighty eastern-flowing river. But Chinese mythology tells a different tale of the Yangtze's origin – a tale of suffering, battles and heroic dragons.

There was a terrible drought, so Heaven sent down two magical dragons – one green, one yellow – to help the people. The dragons discovered that a demon, Wangliang, was to blame.

Crops did not grow on the dry, barren land, and the people faced starvation.

30,000 SHARKS

Chongming Island in the Yangtze delta has a nature reserve and a wetland park. It was there in June 2017 that 30,000 high-fin banded sharks were released into the river to replenish stocks depleted by fishing and pollution.

THE DISAPPEARING SOLDIERS

On 10 December 1939, nearly 3,000 Chinese troops were sent to defend a bridge over the Yangtze against the Japanese. The next morning, they had all vanished. The sentries on the bridge had seen nothing and, to this day, no one knows what happened to the soldiers in Nanjing.

The 'baiji', the Yangtze river dolphin, may already be extinct due to river traffic and fishing.

Huangpu river

The delta islands, created by rocks and sand deposited by the river, slowly shift and change over time.

DIGGING A RIVER

In the 3rd century BCE, the Huangpu river often flooded the lands around it. Lord Chunshen ordered a new course to be dug so that it could flow into the Yangtze. Shanghai, one of the world's largest cities, grew up on the river's banks.

SHANGHAI

HE DOLPHIN GODDESS

young girl was being taken by boat
a market to be sold by her wicked
her. But a great storm blew up and
jumped into the swirling water. The
became a dolphin – the 'Goddess
the Yangtze'.

EAST CHINA SEA

N
W E
S

TAIWAN

PACIFIC OCEAN

Geladaindong Peak

The river drops more than 5km in heigh
in the first 3,000km of its length.

SHRINKING GLACIER

The Yangtze begins as a stream from a glacier on Geladaindong
Peak in the Tanggula mountains of Tibet. Due to human-made
climate change, the glacier is shrinking. It retreated 2m per year in
the 1980s and 1990s, but as much as 6m per year more recently.

Tanggula mountains

TIBET

THE TRAIN THAT TAKES
YOUR BREATH AWAY

In 2006, a railway was built over the Tanggula mountains.
It reaches 5,072m above sea level – the highest point
on any railway in the world. Oxygen is pumped into the
carriages to help passengers breathe more easily.

Tanggula Station is the world's
highest railway station.

Flowing from a tangle of rivers in Peru, the Amazon is surrounded by life in all its wonder. One third of all animal and plant species live in its rainforest. The vegetation on its banks is so thick that not a single bridge has been built across it.

Let's paddle down the river and hear its stories. There is magic in these murky waters and, sometimes, danger . . .

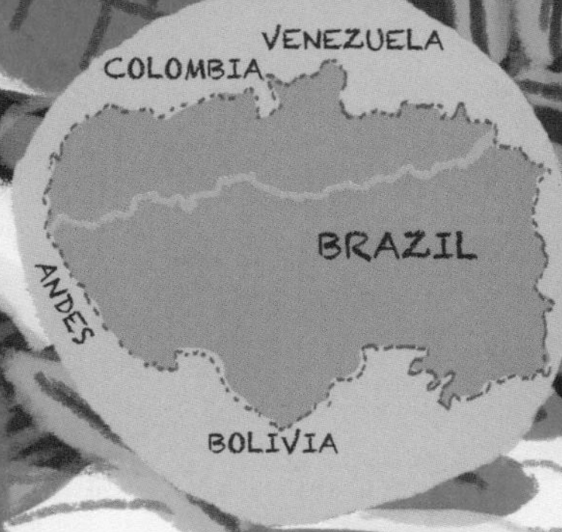

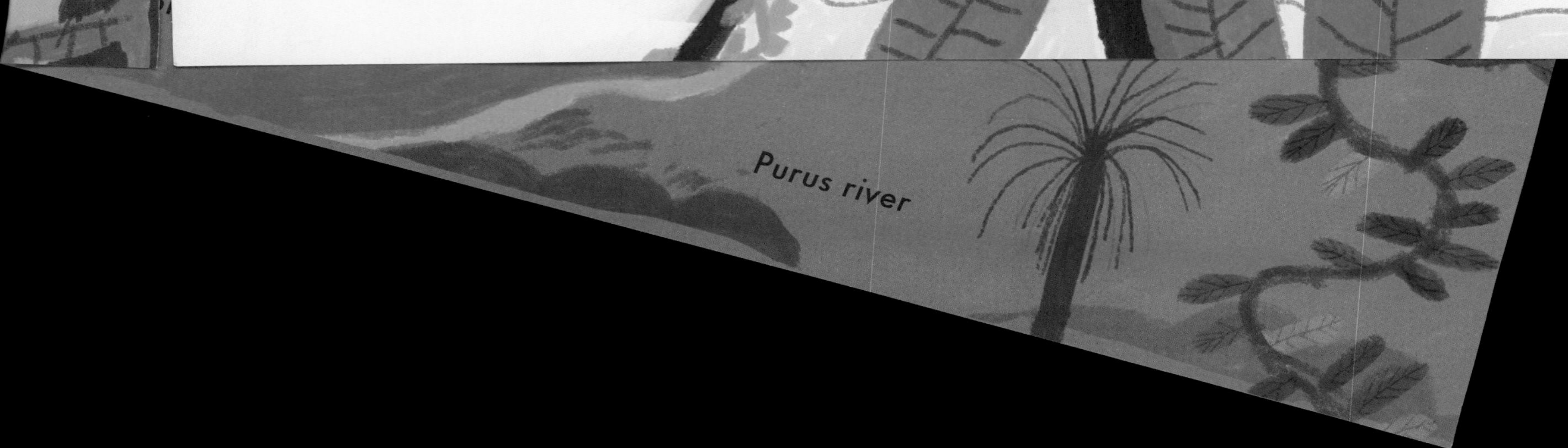

VENEZUELA

COLOMBIA

ANDES

BRAZIL

BOLIVIA

Purus river

The Amazon rainforest, the largest forest in the world at 6 million km2, produces more than 20 per cent of Earth's oxygen.

So Francisco went ahead with 50 men to find food. They found a huge river and built a boat to sail east to the Atlantic. In June 1542, they were attacked by a Tapuya tribe. Its fearsome female warriors reminded Francisco of the Amazons of Greek mythology. Later, King Charles of Spain named the river in their honour – the Amazon.

One story brought Francisco to the river; another gave the river its name. The Amazon breeds stories like the plants that thrive in its thick forests – bright, rich and exotic. Let's dig up some more . . .

The Tapuya women, expert archers, shot arrows deep into the Spaniards' boat.

THE ACCIDENTAL EXPLORER

Francisco de Orellana never intended to be the first European to travel the length of the Amazon river. It was desire for riches and glory that brought the Spaniard to the New World, not exploration. But his search for gold did not go quite as planned.

In 1541, Francisco joined an expedition to hunt for 'El Dorado', a king so wealthy that he covered himself in gold. But if El Dorado had ever existed, he had long since vanished into the jungles of legend. Francisco's disappointed troops were exhausted, disease-ridden and so hungry that they even ate their leather belts.

The expedition also looked for cinnamon trees – exotic spices and plants were valuable goods for trading.

MONSTER SNAKE

Locals sailors would blow conch shells to make sure Yacumama, a monstrous snake 50 paces long, wasn't lurking in the mouth of the river. The beast, said to squirt a powerful jet of water to stun its prey before devouring it, was probably inspired by the anaconda, the world's largest snake.

SURFING THE GREAT ROAR

Every year, a tidal bore sends an Atlantic wave as far as 800km along the Amazon. Up to 4m high and swirling with piranhas, alligators and uprooted trees, the Pororoca ('great roar' in the local Tupi language) attracts daredevil surfers.

FRESH WATER

Every year, the Amazon discharges enough water into the sea to fill 2.6 billion Olympic-size swimming pools! Its water dilutes the Atlantic's saltiness for many kilometres, and sailors have boasted of drinking fresh water before even sighting land.

ATLANTIC OCEAN

Marajo Island

In the Marajoara culture, which flourished from about 400–1350, women were depicted as heroes and shamans who could communicate with the spirit world.

Tapajos river

Fordlandia

THE LOST CITY

In 1930, car-maker Henry Ford set up a new town to produce rubber for tyres. The local workers weren't happy at Fordlandia – football was banned and they had to eat unfamiliar food like hamburgers. They revolted, chasing managers onto boats and the cook into the jungle! Later, the rubber crop failed and the town was abandoned.

IDDEN VILLAGES

remote areas, deforestation has vealed strange circles – ditches rrounding old settlements from e 15th century. The circles prove at people lived all over the forest, smaller streams, and not just xt to the Amazon River.

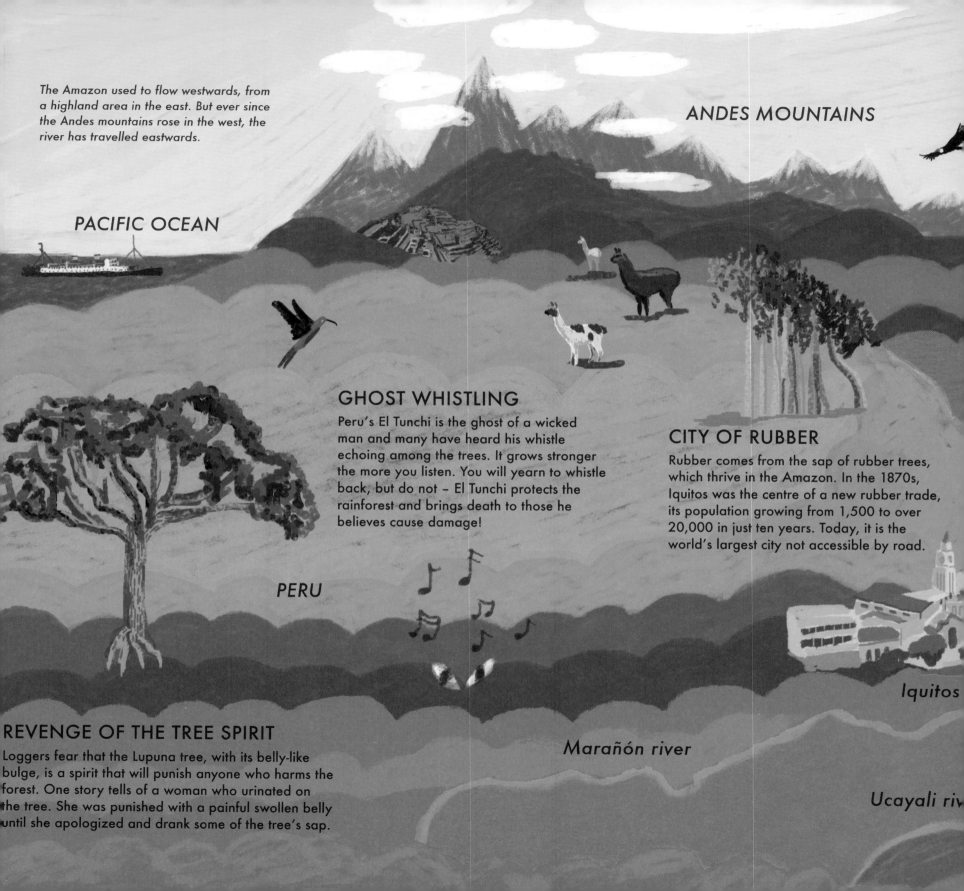

The Amazon used to flow westwards, from a highland area in the east. But ever since the Andes mountains rose in the west, the river has travelled eastwards.

ANDES MOUNTAINS

PACIFIC OCEAN

GHOST WHISTLING

Peru's El Tunchi is the ghost of a wicked man and many have heard his whistle echoing among the trees. It grows stronger the more you listen. You will yearn to whistle back, but do not – El Tunchi protects the rainforest and brings death to those he believes cause damage!

CITY OF RUBBER

Rubber comes from the sap of rubber trees, which thrive in the Amazon. In the 1870s, Iquitos was the centre of a new rubber trade, its population growing from 1,500 to over 20,000 in just ten years. Today, it is the world's largest city not accessible by road.

PERU

Iquitos

REVENGE OF THE TREE SPIRIT

Loggers fear that the Lupuna tree, with its belly-like bulge, is a spirit that will punish anyone who harms the forest. One story tells of a woman who urinated on the tree. She was punished with a painful swollen belly until she apologized and drank some of the tree's sap.

Marañón river

Ucayali riv